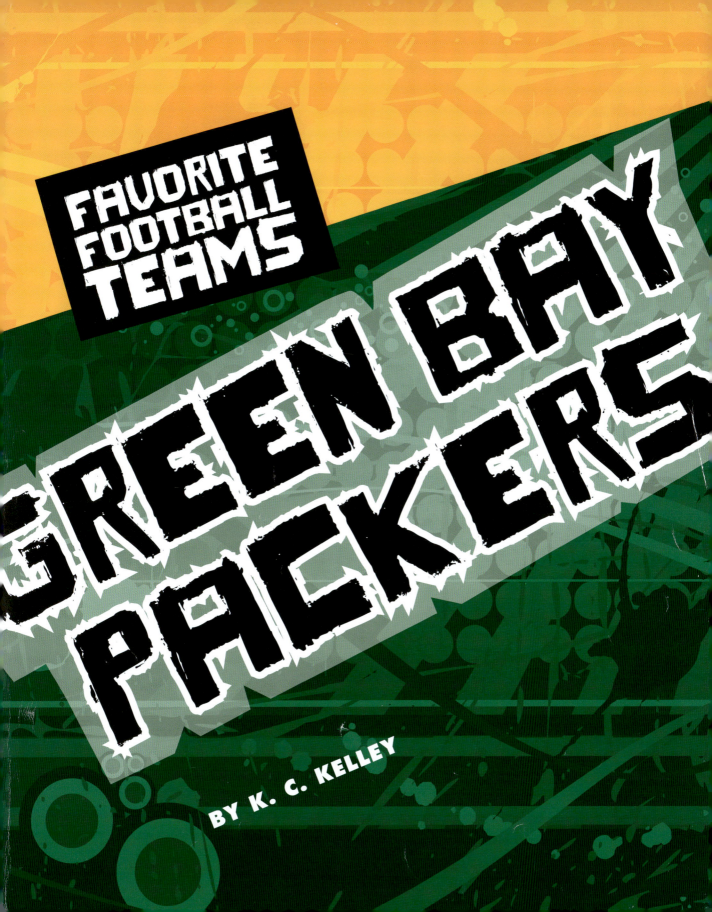

FAVORITE FOOTBALL TEAMS

GREEN BAY PACKERS

BY K. C. KELLEY

The Child's World®

THE CHILD'S WORLD®

1980 Lookout Drive • Mankato, MN 56003-1705
800-599-READ • www.childsworld.com

ACKNOWLEDGMENTS

The Child's World®: Mary Berendes, Publishing Director
Shoreline Publishing Group, LLC: James Buckley, Jr.,
  Production Director
The Design Lab: Kathleen Petelinsek, Design;
  Gregory Lindholm, Page Production

PHOTOS

Cover: Focus on Football
Interior: AP/Wide World: 9, 18, 17;
 Focus on Football: 5, 7, 11, 13, 20, 22, 23, 25, 27;
 Stockexpert: 14

LIBRARY OF CONGRESS
CATALOGING-IN-PUBLICATION DATA

Kelley, K. C.
  Green Bay Packers / by K.C. Kelley.
    p. cm. — (Favorite football teams)
  Includes bibliographical references and index.
  ISBN 978-1-60253-315-8 (library bound : alk. paper)
  1. Green Bay Packers (Football team)—History—Juvenile literature.
I. Title. II. Series.
  GV956.G7K45 2009
  796.332'640977561—dc22   2009009065

Printed in the United States of America
Mankato, Minnesota
November, 2009
PA02026

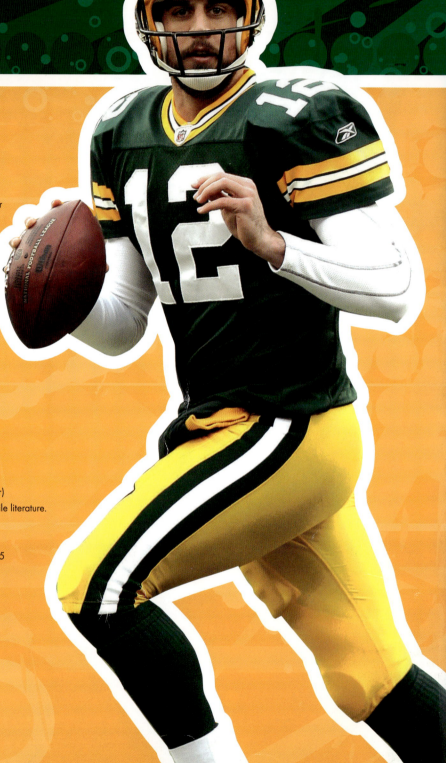

TABLE OF CONTENTS

Go, Packers!

What do the Green Bay Packers pack? They pack their stadium with cheering fans! The Packers are one of the oldest teams in the National Football League (NFL). They have won more championships than any other team. Some of football's greatest players have been Green Bay Packers. The Packers have fans from coast to coast. Let's meet this amazing football team!

Here, the Packers **offense** gathers in a huddle before a play. The **quarterback** is telling his teammates what play they will run.

Who Are the Green Bay Packers?

The Green Bay Packers are one of 32 teams in the NFL. The NFL includes the National Football Conference (NFC) and the American Football Conference (AFC). The Packers play in the North Division of the NFC. The winner of the NFC plays the winner of the AFC in the **Super Bowl**. The Packers have been the NFL champions 12 times!

Pounded by the Pack! Green Bay has a powerful defense, as this New England Patriots player found out.

Where They Came From

Each NFL team is owned by one person—except for the Packers. They are owned by thousands of people! In 1919, the Indian Packing Company in Wisconsin started a pro football team. They hired Curly Lambeau to be their coach. He ran the team for 31 years. He led them to six NFL championships. In 1923, the company sold the team. They sold shares in the team to the people of Green Bay. Today, the people of Green Bay still own the team! In the 1960s, the Packers were great again. They won five more NFL titles.

Coach Curly Lambeau (in overcoat) celebrates with his team after winning the 1944 NFL championship.

10

Who They Play

The Packers play 16 games each season. There are three other teams in the NFC North. They are the Chicago Bears, the Minnesota Vikings, and the Detroit Lions. Every year, the Packers play each of these teams twice. They also play other teams in the NFC and AFC. The Packers and the Bears have been **rivals** since 1923. Their hard-hitting games are always fan favorites!

A pair of NFC North rivals face off across the line of scrimmage. The Packers are taking on the Vikings!

Where They Play

The Packers play their home games at Lambeau Field. It is named for Curly Lambeau, the former coach. The stadium is one of the NFL's oldest. It opened in 1957. Many people think it's the best place to watch an NFL game. The weather is often very cold. Fans and players bundle up to stay warm. The field has heating pipes under the grass. The pipes keep the grass from freezing!

Lambeau Field isn't fancy, but it sure is famous. Some fans wait for years to buy season tickets.

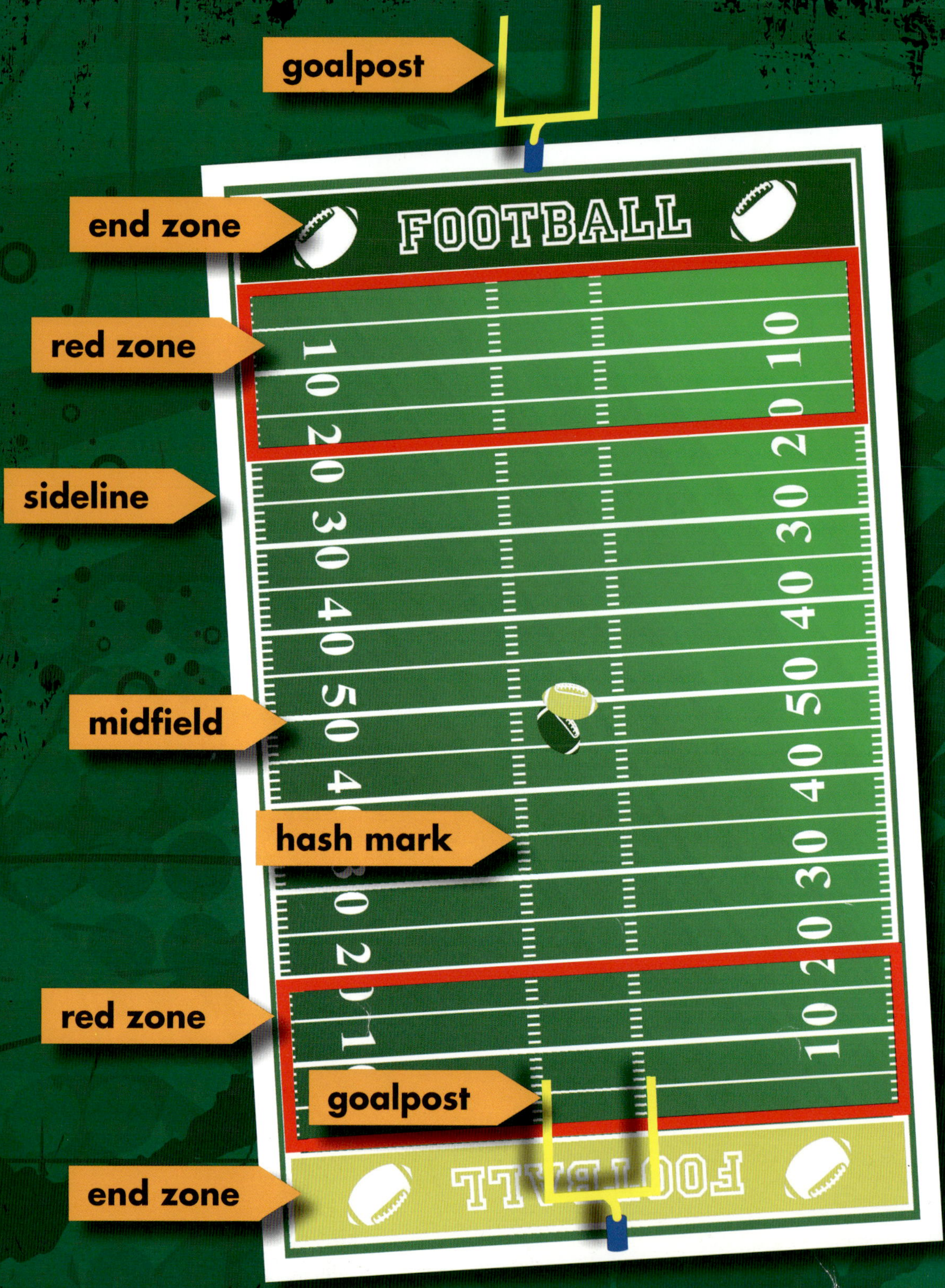

goalpost

end zone

red zone

sideline

midfield

hash mark

red zone

goalpost

end zone

FOOTBALL

10 10
20 20
30 30
40 40
50 50
40 40
30 30
20 20
10 10

14

The Football Field

An NFL field is 100 yards long. At each end is an **end zone** that is another 10 yards deep. Short white **hash marks** on the field mark off every yard. Longer lines mark every five yards. Numbers on the field help fans know where the players are. Goalposts stand at the back of each end zone. On some plays, a team can kick the football through the goalposts to earn points. During the game, each team stands along one sideline of the field. Lambeau Field is covered with real grass. Some indoor NFL stadiums use **artificial**, or fake, grass.

During a game, the two teams stand on the sidelines. They usually stand near midfield, waiting for their turns to play. Coaches walk on the sidelines, too, along with cheerleaders and photographers.

Big Days!

The Green Bay Packers have had many great moments in their long history. Here are three of the greatest:

1929: The Packers won 12 games and tied one. They didn't lose any games, and they won their first NFL championship.

1967: On January 15, the Packers won the first Super Bowl. They beat the Kansas City Chiefs 35–10.

1997: On January 26, Green Bay returned to the top of the NFL. They won another Super Bowl. They beat the New England Patriots 35–21.

Yee-ha! Brett Favre races down the field to celebrate a touchdown during Super Bowl XXXI in 1997.

17

Tough Days!

The Packers can't win all their games. Some games or seasons don't turn out well. The players keep trying to play their best, though! Here are some painful memories from Packers history:

1958: The Packers had their worst season ever. They lost 10 games, while winning only one and tying another.

1980: The Packers hate to lose to the Bears. On December 7 this year, they got crushed. Chicago beat them 61 – 7.

2007: Great quarterback Brett Favre retired after 16 seasons with the Packers. Later, he changed his mind and played again. He joined the New York Jets in 2008.

Brett Favre left the field as a Packer for the last time in 2007. Green Bay fans were sad to lose such a popular and successful player.

Meet the Fans

Green Bay Packers fans have a great nickname. They are called "Cheeseheads." Their home state of Wisconsin makes a lot of cheese. Some Packers fans wear foam hats that look like cheese! These fans look silly, but they love their football team. Packers fans put up with ice, snow, rain, and cold to cheer. Green Bay families often go to Packers games together. When players do well, they jump into the stands. This is called the "Lambeau Leap." It's named for the stadium.

After scoring a touchdown, Ruvell Martin does the "Lambeau Leap." The fans grab and hug him and celebrate his great play.

Heroes Then . . .

The Packers are one of the NFL's oldest teams. Their list of heroes is almost as long as their football field! **Receiver** Don Hutson set many records and helped the team win three NFL titles. Quarterback Bart Starr led the team in the 1960s. He was a Super Bowl Most Valuable Player twice!

Linebacker Ray Nitschke looked mean . . . and he played mean! He was one of the best ever at his position. Quarterback Brett Favre starred for the Packers from 1992 through 2007. He had more touchdown passes and passing yards than any other NFL quarterback.

1959–1967

VINCE LOMBARDI
Coach

Bart Starr (left) played for the famous coach Vince Lombardi (right). Lombardi was tough and smart—and one of the best coaches in NFL history.

Heroes Now . . .

Aaron Rodgers had big shoes to fill. He took over as quarterback after Brett Favre left in 2008. Rodgers did very well. He threw 28 touchdown passes and passed for more than 4,000 yards. Many of those throws went to receiver Greg Jennings. **Cornerback** Charles Woodson joined Green Bay in 2006. He is one of the best at his position. He has played in five **Pro Bowls**. **Defensive end** Aaron Kampman loves to **sack** the quarterback. He has had at least 10 sacks in two seasons.

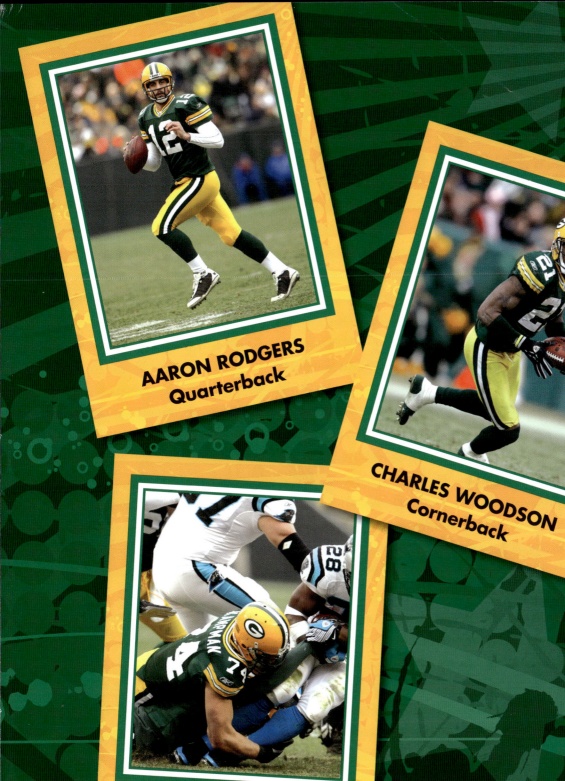

AARON RODGERS
Quarterback

CHARLES WOODSON
Cornerback

AARON KAMPMAN
Defensive End

25

Gearing Up

Green Bay Packers players wear lots of gear to help keep them safe. They wear pads from head to toe. Check out this picture of Aaron Rodgers and learn what NFL players wear.

The Football

NFL footballs are made of four pieces of leather. White laces help the quarterback grip and throw the ball. Inside the football is a rubber bag that holds air.

Football Fact

NFL footballs don't have white lines around them. Only college teams use footballs with those lines.

helmet

facemask

shoulder pad

chest pad

hand warmer

thigh pad

knee pad

cleats

27

Sports Stats

Note: All numbers are through the 2008 season.

Touchdowns

TOUCHDOWN MAKERS

These players have scored the most touchdowns for the Packers.

PLAYER	TOUCHDOWNS
Don Hutson	105
Jim Taylor	91

PASSING FANCY

Top Packers quarterbacks

PLAYER	PASSING YARDS
Brett Favre	61,655
Bart Starr	24,718

Quarterbacks

RUN FOR GLORY

Top Packers running backs

PLAYER	RUSHING YARDS
Jim Taylor	8,207
Ahman Green	8,162

Running backs

GREEN BAY PACKERS

Receivers

CATCH A STAR
Top Packers receivers

PLAYER	CATCHES
Sterling Sharpe	595
Donald Driver	577

TOP DEFENDERS
Packers defensive records

Most **interceptions**: Bobby Dillon, 52
Most sacks: Kabeer Gbaja-Biamila, 74.5

Defenders

COACH
Most Coaching Wins

Curly Lambeau, 212

Coach

29

Glossary

artificial fake, not real

cornerback a player who covers the other team's receivers and tries to keep them from making catches

defense players who are trying to keep the other team from scoring

defensive end a player who tries to tackle the other team's quarterback and running backs

end zone a 10-yard deep area at each end of the field

hash marks short white lines that mark off each yard on the football field

interceptions catches made by defensive players

linebacker a defensive player who begins each play standing behind the main defensive line

line of scrimmage the place where the two teams face off when a play starts

offense players who have the ball and are trying to score

Pro Bowls the NFL's annual all-star game, played in February in Hawaii

quarterback the key offensive player who starts each play and passes or hands off to a teammate

receiver an offensive player who catches forward passes

rivals teams that play each other often and have an ongoing competition

running backs offensive players who run with the football and catch passes

sack a tackle of a quarterback behind the line of scrimmage

Super Bowl the NFL's annual championship game

touchdown a six-point score made by carrying or catching the ball in the end zone

Find Out More

BOOKS

Buckley, James Jr. *The Scholastic Ultimate Book of Football*. New York: Scholastic, 2009.

Madden, John, and Bill Gutman. *Heroes of Football*. New York: Dutton, 2006.

Polzer, Tim. *Play Football! A Guide for Young Players from the National Football League*. New York: DK Publishing, 2002.

Sandler, Michael. *Brett Favre: Football Heroes Making a Difference*. New York: Bearport Publishing, 2009.

Stewart, Mark. *The Green Bay Packers*. Chicago: Norwood House Press, 2007.

WEB SITE

Visit our Web site for lots of links about the Green Bay Packers and other NFL football teams:

childsworld.com/links

Note to Parents, Teachers, and Librarians: We routinely verify our Web links to make sure they are safe, active sites—so encourage your readers to check them out!

Index

About the Author

K. C. Kelley is a huge football fan! He has written dozens of books on football and other sports for young readers. K. C. used to work for NFL Publishing and has covered several Super Bowls.